Overcoming Obstacles:
Sports Biographies

Flo Jo:
The Story of
Florence Griffith Joyner

by
Alan Venable

Don Johnston Incorporated
Volo, Illinois

Edited by:

Jerry Stemach, MS, CCC-SLP
Speech/Language Pathologist, Director of Content Development, Start-to-Finish® Books

Gail Portnuff Venable, MS, CCC-SLP
Speech/Language Pathologist, San Francisco, California

Dorothy Tyack, MA
Learning Disabilities Specialist, San Francisco, California

Consultant:

Ted S. Hasselbring, PhD
William T. Brian Professor of Special Education Technology, University of Kentucky

Graphics and Illustrations:

Photographs and illustrations are all created professionally
and modified to provide the best possible support for the
intended reader.

Narration:

Professional actors and actresses read the text to build
excitement and to model research-based elements of fluency:
intonation, stress, prosody, phrase groupings and rate.
The rate has been set to maximize comprehension for the reader.

Published by:

Don Johnston Incorporated
26799 West Commerce Drive
Volo, IL 60073

800.999.4660 USA Canada
800.889.5242 Technical Support
www.donjohnston.com

DON JOHNSTON

International Standard Book Number
ISBN 1-893376-44-3

Contents

Chapter 1

Race the Rabbit

If you want to do something with your life, start now! In 1988, Florence Griffith Joyner became the fastest woman runner in the world. How old was she when she started racing? Five years old. She didn't know that she was going to become an Olympic star. She just knew that she liked to run.

Florence was born in 1959 in Los Angeles, California. She had ten sisters and brothers. Florence's family called her Dee Dee.

Dee Dee's father worked for an airline. After Dee Dee was born, her father got a new job at an airline in the Mojave Desert, so the family moved there. The Mojave Desert is also in California.

Dee Dee's mother didn't want to raise her children in the desert. Dee Dee's mother was very beautiful. She had gone to Los Angeles when she was young to see if she could be a model. That dream had not come true, but she still wanted to live in L.A.

Dee Dee's parents got a divorce. When Dee Dee was four years old, her mother moved the kids back to L.A. They had no money, so they moved to a housing project in a part of L.A. that is called Watts. A lot of people who are poor live in Watts.

Watts was rough. It was a hard place to grow up. It was not where Dee Dee's family wanted to live. When they moved to Watts, Dee Dee's mother told the children, "Life is like a baby. A baby comes into the world without anything.

Then it starts crawling. Then it stands up. Then it takes its first step and it starts walking. So start walking!"

Sometimes little Dee Dee saw that her mother was sad.

"This is not home," her mother would say. "I just want to get you out of here."

Dee Dee's family was poor, but they didn't feel poor. They were a strong family and they took care of each other. Their mother kept her eye on the children and supported them in every way that she could.

She did sewing jobs to make a living. She taught Dee Dee how to sew, also. Dee Dee liked to sew.

Sometimes the children visited their father in the Mojave Desert. When Dee Dee was five, she stayed with him for about a year. There were jackrabbits in the desert. A jackrabbit is big, with very long ears and long back feet. Dee Dee's father knew that she liked to run. He asked her if she could race a jackrabbit. So Dee Dee started chasing the rabbits around.

Pretty soon, people said that she could run as fast as a jackrabbit. She was faster than the boys.

One of her sisters remembers how fast little Dee Dee could run. She says that Dee Dee was like lightning.

Chapter 2

The Snake

When Dee Dee was seven, she joined a sports program for kids in Watts. Now she could be in real races with other kids. The program was led by a famous boxer named Sugar Ray Robinson. Dee Dee's mother thought it was a great idea.

When Dee Dee was little, she didn't think much about winning a race. "It was fun for me," she said. "It didn't matter if I won or lost. I felt like a winner as long as I did my best. My mother helped me to see things that way."

Dee Dee liked other things besides running. Her grandmother showed her how to paint fingernails and braid hair. Dee Dee braided the hair of all the other girls that she knew. She braided her own hair, also. One day, she made a braid that stuck straight up on the top of her head. Other kids thought Dee Dee looked silly and teased her about it. She just laughed.

Dee Dee's mother was strict. The kids were not allowed to watch TV all week. So Dee Dee sewed and knitted.

She read books. She wrote a diary.
She wrote poems. Her mind was
always busy.

Dee Dee always thought for herself.
When she got older, she wanted her
own pet. Dee Dee thought that the
family dog had too many fleas, so Dee
Dee got a snake and named it Brandy.
Brandy was a boa constrictor that grew
to be five feet long.

Dee Dee loved Brandy. "I bathed
her and put lotion on her," she said.

"Every week I would go down to the pet shop and get some mice or rats, and feed them to Brandy. When Brandy shed her skin, I saved it and painted it different colors."

One time, Dee Dee was walking around a mall with Brandy wrapped around her neck and the guards at the mall made her leave. They said that Dee Dee was scaring people.

You might think that Dee Dee was very sure of herself. But really she was shy. Some people are like that.

They do wild things on the outside, but inside they feel that they should stay quiet and not get too close to other people. When Dee Dee was little, Sugar Ray Robinson came to a race to give out the medals. When he gave a medal to Dee Dee, she was too shy to look at him.

Sometimes Dee Dee didn't talk to other kids, so they thought that she was being a snob. When she did something strange, like wear a snake around her neck, they thought that she was showing off.

Dee Dee wasn't being a snob and she wasn't showing off. She was just being herself. She was quiet because she was shy.

Chapter 3

Two High School Runners

Florence "Dee Dee" Griffith went to high school in Watts. She got good grades and joined the track and field team. Track events are races that are run around a track. Field events are held on the field inside the track. Two of the field events are the long jump and the high jump.

The other kids on the track and field team liked Florence. One of them said, "We all knew that she was awfully fast, but she was always down to earth. She never acted like she was better than anyone else."

Florence's friends on the track and field team didn't think that she was a snob.

A short, fast race is called a sprint. Florence was mainly a sprinter. She ran the 100-yard dash. One hundred yards is the length of an American football field. She also ran in longer races and in relay team races. A relay team has four runners. In a 100-yard relay, each runner runs 100 yards. One runner starts the race. She carries a stick that is called a baton.

After 100 yards, she gives the baton to the next runner, who runs another 100 yards. The baton is passed until each runner has run her part of the race.

Florence was also in the long jump. For this event, you start by running. Then you jump and see how far you can go in the air before you hit the ground. You land in a pit of sand so that you don't get hurt.

By the age of 14, Florence was winning medals in U.S. high school track events. Her school's relay team was state champion in California.

Florence was also getting all A's in school. She was a hero there.

Florence was fast. She was faster than most of the boys. But there was another female high school runner in Watts who was even faster than Florence. Her name was Valerie Brisco.

Valerie's older brother Robert had been on the track team at a different high school in Watts. One day, Robert was out practicing on the track.

Suddenly, a stray bullet hit and killed him. Valerie was 14 years old when Robert died. His death made Valerie decide to start running. She did it to remember her brother.

Chapter 4

Going to College

In 1978, Florence went to college. She wanted to study business. She chose a branch of the California State University that was near L.A. People called this college "Cal State."

At first, Florence did not go out for track at Cal State because she didn't have time. She wanted to study hard. She had a job in a bank to help support her family and pay for school. But the track coach wanted her to run. The coach's name was Bobby Kersee.

He had other good runners like Valerie Brisco, but he wanted Florence, also. So Florence decided to give it a try.

Track was different in college. When Florence was in high school, the races were measured in yards. But in college, the races were measured in meters. A yard is 36 inches long and a meter is about 39 inches long. A 100-meter race is about the same as 109 yards. The shortest college sprint is 100 meters. College runners can run 100 meters in about 11 seconds.

Is that fast? Try it and see! That's about 10 yards in one second! There's also another sprint that is 200 meters long.

The Cal State runners were all very fast. Some had a chance to get a place on the U.S. Olympic team. It was not hard for Florence to be the best sprinter at her high school. But it was hard for her to be the best sprinter at Cal State!

Florence's roommate at Cal State was another sprinter who had run against Florence in high school.

She didn't think that Florence was the greatest runner. This other sprinter said, "A lot of athletes come and go. But what I did notice was Florence's white tights. And her hair was slicked back. I said, 'Who's that girl with the white tights?'"

Back then, runners didn't look flashy. The men and women wore whatever their team was wearing. At practice, they wore old sweatsuits. But Florence had to be different. She was beautiful and she didn't hide it.

She had long fingernails, and she liked to paint them. The other women didn't like this. They wanted to fit in more with the men because back then sports were still mainly for men. The women didn't want people to be thinking, "Who's that girl with the pretty tights?"

Florence didn't run well in her first year at college. She had hurt a tendon in her leg. A tendon is a part of the body that connects a muscle to a bone. But the tendon wasn't her biggest problem. Her real problem was money.

CORBIS/Neal Preston

Florence with her long fingernails.

Florence didn't have enough money for her second year of college. She would have to quit school until she had worked and saved more money.

Bobby Kersee found out about Florence's problem. He didn't want her to quit school. He helped her to get loans and scholarship money from Cal State. He got her back into college.

Then Bobby Kersee left Cal State. He got hired as the new track coach at UCLA. UCLA stands for University of California at Los Angeles. UCLA also had a very good track team.

When Kersee moved, he asked Valerie and Florence to go there with him. Bobby Kersee was a very good coach, so the two women transferred from Cal State to UCLA to stay with him.

Chapter 5

Getting Stronger

CORBIS/Reuters

Florence on the running track, wearing white tights.

The Summer Olympics are held every four years. By the time of the 1980 Olympics, Florence was 20 years old. Her tendon had healed so she could race again.

A few months before every Olympics, there is a track meet in the United States that is called the Olympic trials. The trials decide who will be on the U.S. Olympic team. Florence and Valerie went to the trials and ran in the 200-meter race. The three fastest runners would make the team. Valerie made it but Florence came in fourth.

So Florence didn't make the Olympic team in 1980. The only thing that she won at the trials was a look from one of the men on the team. His name was Al Joyner. He thought that Florence was beautiful. Al and Florence would meet again.

Florence was getting faster. She was learning some secrets about track that no one had taught her in high school.

Running races is not as simple as it looks. Each type of race is a little different.

The 100-meter sprint is run on a straight track. There are no turns. But the 200-meter sprint is run partly around the curve of the track. Running fast around a curve is tricky because you need to keep your left shoulder a little ahead of your right shoulder. You also need to use your legs differently as you go around the curve. There is a lot to learn about running!

In the next three years, Florence ran in lots of races in the United States and in Europe. She ran in races that were 100, 200, and 400 meters long.

CORBIS/Bettmann-UPI

Florence runs in the 100-meter sprint.

In 1982, she won a big national race in the 200-meter sprint. Florence also ran well on relay teams.

Florence loved running at UCLA. "The team was so much fun," she said. "We'd get together for Bobby's birthday. We'd chip in to buy him a suit, to make him look nice at the meets."

Florence's fingernails got longer and longer. She painted them with rainbow colors. Some other UCLA runners didn't think that this was right.

In a relay race, the runners have to pass the baton while they are running. Long fingernails might get in the way and make someone drop the baton. Then the whole team would lose the race.

One of her teammates told her, "We all know that you're different, Florence, but why do you have to show it all the time?"

But Florence wouldn't cut her nails.

Chapter 6

As Good as Silver

REUTERS/CORBIS-Bettmann

Florence wins her 200-meter heat at the Olympics to get into the final race.

Florence finished college in 1983. She worked at a bank during the day and practiced running at night. She was training for the 1984 Olympics. Florence thought that 1984 could be her big year. Those Olympics would be held in L.A. The U.S. Olympic trials would be held in L.A., also. Florence got busy and sewed some great running suits!

Florence practiced hard. At the trials she wore the shiny new running suits that she had made.

They were bright-colored suits like the kind that speed skaters wore. The suits glowed in the sun. People stared at Florence. She was just too gorgeous!

Al Joyner was trying out for an event called the triple jump. The triple jump is like the long jump. You start out running, and then you take one hop, one step, and one long jump.

Al looked across the field at Florence and thought, "That Florence Griffith is still the most beautiful woman that I ever saw!"

Florence ran in the 200-meter event at the trials and came in second. This time she had made it onto the U.S. team!

At the Olympics, Florence was not allowed to wear her own clothes. She had to wear the U.S. Olympic uniform. But she could paint her long fingernails! She painted one red, the next one white, and the next one blue. She painted the fourth one gold because gold was the color of a first place medal.

Athletes come to the Olympics from all around the world. There are many runners in each event. They can't all run in one race together, so they are divided into heats. A heat is a group of runners who run against each other. In each round of heats, the runners who come in first and second get to move on to another heat. If you don't come in first or second in a heat, you can't be in the final event at the Olympics. In 1982, Florence won a big national race in the 200 meters.

Florence also ran well on relay teams. At the Olympics, there can be two or three rounds of heats before the final race for the medals. The heats that are just before the final race are called the semi-finals.

Florence ran well in the 200-meter heats and she got to the semi-finals. She won the semi-finals and got to the final race. Can you guess who won the gold medal? It was Valerie Brisco from the old UCLA team. Florence came in second.

REUTERS/CORBIS-Bettmann

Florence hands the baton to her teammate in a relay race.

She felt proud of winning the silver medal, but of course she had wanted the gold.

Florence had one more shot at the gold medal in the 1984 Olympics. She asked the U.S. team officers to let her run in the 400-meter relay. But her fingernails were longer than ever. The officers shook their heads, and said, "You can't run unless you cut your nails."

Then Florence shook *her* head. She wouldn't cut her nails. So the relay team ran without her, and they won the gold medal anyway.

Al Joyner went home with the gold medal in the triple jump. He was still thinking about Florence Griffith, but she didn't know it yet.

Chapter 7

Back to Work!

CORBIS/Neal Preston

Florence at home.

Florence didn't feel like running after the 1984 Olympics. She felt low. She kept on training, but not very hard. She went back to her job. She also made money by painting other women's nails and braiding their hair. She made up new styles of braiding that took hours to finish. She ate too much. Now she was gaining pounds instead of speed.

Bobby Kersee scolded her. "You have the mind of a champion," he told her. "So get back in shape. I know that you can do it."

Early in 1986, Al Joyner came out to
live in L.A. and to train with his sister.
His sister was Jackie Joyner. Jackie
had been one of Florence's teammates
at UCLA. In 1986, Jackie Joyner
married Bobby Kersee and became
Jackie Joyner-Kersee.

Al had another reason for moving
out to L.A. He hadn't forgotten
Florence. They saw each other at
practice. He started spending time
with her. He was positive and helpful.
Florence liked him and they got along
well.

CORBIS/REUTERS

Florence is lifted up by Al Joyner after she wins a race.

He was like a friend or an older brother, and he helped her to get her mind back into running.

Florence began to train in a new way. She spent more time lifting weights. The weights would build up her muscles. She also ran long distances. Most sprinters didn't practice that way. They didn't think that running for miles was good training for sprinters. But Florence was always different.

The training began to pay off. At the start of a sprint, a runner puts her feet against two starting blocks. The blocks are set on the track so that they do not move. The runner gets a fast start by pushing off the blocks. Florence's new strength gave her a faster start. It built up her speed. Her sprints got faster.

In the spring of 1987, Florence got back into serious racing. By June, she was faster than Al Joyner at 100 meters.

One night in July, Al rented a limo and took Florence for a ride. Inside the limo, he got down on his knees and asked her to marry him. Florence was so amazed that she didn't know what to say.

The next day, Florence and Al were at a pizza place. Her little nephew Larry was with them. So was her niece, Khalisha. Larry won a prize while playing a game called "Skee Ball." The prize was a little yellow charm that said "Y-E-S."

Khalisha grabbed the charm and gave it to her aunt Florence. Khalisha said, "You can't keep him waiting!"

"Khalisha!" said Florence. "You're only 10 years old!"

Then Florence thought, "Al is patient with me, and he's honest. Maybe he's too honest sometimes! But the longer we know each other, the more we have in common."

Florence gave the charm to Al. That was how she said, "Yes."

"It's about time!" cried Khalisha. "You're lucky that he still wants you!"

At the World Track Meet in Rome in August 1987, Florence helped the U.S. win the 400-meter relay. She came in second in the 200 meters. She was beaten by a runner from East Germany.

In October, Florence and Al were married. Now her name was Florence Griffith Joyner. Al said, "She's the smartest, sweetest, most beautiful woman in the world. I can't believe that she married me."

After the wedding, life was very busy. Al and Florence both had jobs and trained at night. Florence wrote poems and painted nails and braided hair. Time was tight, but Florence felt more relaxed. That was good. If you want to win, you can't be tense about it all the time. You have to train hard, but you also have to relax.

Chapter 8

Amazing Times

CORBIS/Wolfgang Kaehler

In 1988, the Olympics were held in Korea.

Runners race against other runners. They also race against the clock. They want to break all the records by beating the fastest time. When someone breaks a world record, the new world record is often just a few 100ths of a second faster than the old record. Think about taking one second and dividing it into 100 parts!

The 1988 Olympics were held in September in Korea. The U.S. trials were held in July in the state of Indiana.

Florence took 14 new running suits to the trials. She wanted to look great even if she lost. Some of her suits had tights that covered just one leg. The other leg was bare. Florence got this idea one day when she made a mistake and cut off one leg of a pair of colored tights. She liked her mistake. That one colored leg looked wild! "Colors excite me," she told Al.

Indiana is hot in the summer. It was 98 degrees. Heat can be good for sprinters. It makes their muscles loose.

Before the trials, the women's world record for 100 meters was held by Evelyn Ashford. Her time was 10.76 seconds. Ashford was at the trials. People asked, "Will Ashford break her own world record?"

But there was a problem at the trials. There was too much wind. A wind that blows on the back of a runner is called a tailwind. Even a little tailwind can speed up a sprinter. If the tailwind is faster than 2 meters per second, a sprint time doesn't count as a world record.

Most experts didn't think that Florence would be a star at the trials. They thought that she might get on the team in the 200 meters, but not in the 100 meters. They didn't know what Bob Kersee knew. He had timed Florence in June. Her 100-meter time was only 10.89 seconds. It was only one-tenth of a second behind the world record.

When Florence came out on the track for the 100-meter event, she was wearing bright green tights that had only one leg. Her hair was long. Her nails were orange, black, and white.

In the first heat, she won with a time of 10.60 seconds. That was faster than the old world record! But it didn't count because there was too much tailwind.

For the next round, Florence wore one leg tights again. This time the tights were purple and blue.

CORBIS/Bettmann

Florence Griffith Joyner and a teammate at the U.S. Olympic trials in Indiana.

Bobby told her to test the wind right before the race. If the air was still, she should try for the record. If there was wind, she should save her strength for later races.

When the starting gun went off, Florence did not feel any wind. She ran as fast as she could. She won her heat in 10.49 seconds!

"Incredible!" the announcer shouted.

Bobby Kersee was amazed. He said, "I had my camera on her, and she ran out of the picture!"

Even Florence didn't believe it at first. Her time was more than two tenths of a second faster than Ashford's world record.

Some people in the crowd said, "It must be the wind."

But the wind was very gusty that day. Sometimes it blew forward. Then it blew back. Then it blew sideways. The officials checked the machines that measured the wind. During Florence's heat, there had been no tailwind. Florence Griffith Joyner had set a new world record!

The crowd could not believe it.

The semi-finals were on the next day. The air was still. Florence came out in a black, two-leg suit. She ran far ahead of all the others. Her time was 10.70 seconds. This time was also faster that Ashford's world record.

In the final race, Florence and Ashford lined up side by side. Florence sprang out into the lead. She finished 3 meters ahead of Ashford with a time of 10.61 seconds. Now everyone could see that this woman was as fast as lightning!

The 200-meter sprint was next. The U.S. record was 21.81 seconds. That record was held by Valerie Brisco. In the finals, Florence wore a body suit of white lace. When the event was over, she had won the race and set a new U.S. record of 21.77 seconds!

Who was this woman? She was so beautiful, and so fast and free! From then on, reporters called her "Flo Jo."

Chapter 9

1988: The Final Test

UPI/CORBIS-Bettmann

Florence, wearing a lace body suit, stands with another teammate at the 1988 Olympic trials.

Florence talked about how she felt as she got ready to go to the 1988 Olympics in Korea. "When you get to the Olympic Games, it's more mental than physical. You can't train anymore. You're just waiting to perform. You've got to stay focused on what you are there to do. You've got to want to go out there and do it."

Florence and Al took a plane to Korea. In the airport, Al's baggage cart fell on Florence's ankle. For several days she couldn't practice. She put ice on her ankle.

She prayed. She stretched. She stayed off her feet. By the time the sprint races began, her ankle seemed OK.

In Korea, Florence had to prove herself again by facing sprinters from East Germany. The East Germans were very fast. Their star sprinter held the world record in the 200 meters. She was four inches taller than Flo Jo.

Florence couldn't wear her famous suits this time. She had to dress like the rest of her team.

CORBIS/REUTERS

Florence runs in her heat of the women's 100-meter sprint.

But it didn't matter. In the 100 meters, she was the best. Florence beat the tall East German star and she broke Valerie Brisco's Olympic record.

In the 200 meters, the world record was 21.71 seconds. In the semi-finals of this race, Florence broke the record with a time of 21.56 seconds. In the finals, she won the gold medal.

Then Flo Jo ran in the 100-meter relay race and won another gold medal.

Flo Jo also ran in the 400-meter relay. But this time a Russian team was faster. The Russians set a new world record. Flo's team came in second.

There was a question about Florence's medals. Ten other athletes had to leave the Olympics because they had been using a drug called a steroid. Steroids make bodies grow faster and stronger, but these drugs are not allowed in the Olympics. Some people thought that Flo Jo must be using drugs, also.

But Flo Jo had taken many tests, and all of the tests had shown that there were no drugs in her body.

Florence was the first American woman to win four medals at the same Olympic Games. She won three gold medals and one silver medal. She had set another new world record. Her two world records were going to last for many years.

Chapter 10

The Sudden End

REUTERS/CORBIS-Bettmann

Florence Griffith Joyner carries the American flag after winning an Olympic gold medal.

Florence Griffith Joyner got many awards after the Olympics. She also had many other plans for the rest of her life. She designed athletic clothing for stores. She wrote about sports in the newspaper. She talked about sports on TV. She acted in movies.

Florence went back to Watts to talk with students and help them to get a strong start in life. She set up a new track program for kids that was like the program that she had been in as a child.

CORBIS/Neal Preston

Flo Jo and Al Joyner with their daughter Mary Ruth.

In 1991, Flo Jo and Al had a baby girl. They named her Mary Ruth Joyner. Soon Mary was running, also. People called her "Mo Jo."

Then Flo Jo decided to go back to running. She couldn't get in shape in time for the 1992 Olympics, so she aimed for 1996. She wanted to set a new record in the 400 meters and she wanted to run in the marathon, the longest Olympic race. The marathon is 26 miles long.

Florence told herself, "I haven't competed in the Olympic Games since 1988, but so what? My desire is still there. Stay focused. It's what I want to do." In 1995, she made a video that told about reaching goals in life.

But Florence was older now. Training was harder. She hurt a tendon in her foot and missed the 1996 Olympics.

She wrote a book called *Running for Dummies* because she wanted to teach other people how to run.

Florence wins another race, wearing one of her famous outfits that covers just one leg.

While she was writing the book, she kept on training for the next Olympic Games.

In September 1998, Al Joyner went out of the house for a little while one evening. When he came back, he found Florence lying in bed. Her face was pressed against the pillow. She was dead. She was only 38 years old.

No one knows for sure how Florence died. The doctors think that she had a disease called epilepsy. Sometimes epilepsy causes bad seizures.

In a seizure, your brain sends many orders to the rest of your body all at once. Your muscles can get very tense and pull against each other. Some people have blackouts during a seizure. A blackout is like suddenly falling asleep. Sometimes people die from a seizure.

At Florence's funeral, Al cried and talked to her. He said, "Hello, honey, Dee Dee, Flo Jo, Florence, Honey Bun, my loving wife. I told you a long time ago how much I loved you."

Flo Jo with Mary Ruth in 1992.

CORBIS/Neal Preston

Mary Ruth sang a song for her mother.

All over the country, people cried when Florence Griffith Joyner died. In Watts, people cried because she had been like a wonderful member of everyone's family.

Florence Griffith Joyner proved important things to the world. She proved that a poor young girl from Watts could become the fastest runner in the world. She showed how people can have many dreams and interests, not just in sports.

She showed that a strong person can be beautiful, and a beautiful person can be strong.

So think about all of your own dreams for tomorrow and start work on those dreams today.

The End

About the Writer

Alan Venable was born in Pittsburgh, Pennsylvania in 1944. After graduating from Harvard, he taught classes in East Africa for several years and traveled in Africa and Asia.

In later years, he studied and taught creative writing and children's literature at several colleges. In addition to his many books in the Start-to-Finish™ series, he has written several books of fiction for children, as well as plays and novels for adults.

Alan lives in San Francisco and is married to Gail Venable, a speech and language clinician and one of the editors of the Start-to-Finish™ series. He and Gail have two children, Morgan and Noe.

About the Reader

Denise Jordan-Walker was a radio announcer in Chicago for over 15 years before she started a company called the Jordan Walker Entertainment Group in 1994. The company works with other companies to produce projects in music, sports, film, theater and publishing.

The Jordan Walker Entertainment Group is now a national company that has introduced many popular writers and entertainers to the public.

A Note from the Start-to-Finish® Editors

This book has been divided into approximately equal short chapters so that the student can read a chapter and take the cloze test in one reading session. This length constraint has sometimes required the authors and editors to make transitions in mid-chapter or to break up chapters in unexpected places.

You will also notice that Start-to-Finish Books look different from other high-low readers and chapter books. The text layout of this book coordinates with the other media components (CD and audiocassette) of the Start-to-Finish series.

The text in the book matches, line for line and page for page, the text shown on the computer screen, enabling readers to follow along easily in the book. Each page ends in a complete sentence so that the student can either practice the page (repeat reading) or turn the page to continue with the story. If the next sentence cannot fit on the page in its entirety, it has been shifted to the next page. For this reason, the sentence at the top of a page may not be indented, signaling that it is part of the paragraph from the preceding page.

Words are not hyphenated at the ends of lines. This sometimes creates extra space at the end of a line, but eliminates confusion for the struggling reader.